Praise for Melody Prado

'The Devil wears Prada and cats read Prado. Fssst!'

Cosmopawlitan

'The ultimate self-help book for cats, human training made easy'

Daily Meow

'A fascinating study to understand human behaviour and cat power, this book is a comprehensive look at the feline-human relationship, and will certainly appeal to all cats'

Marie Cat

'Deliciously filled with wit and style'

The Meow York Times

'Captivating, you won't be able to put it down'

The Sydney Morning Purr

HOW TO
INFLUENCE YOUR HUMAN
AND
WIN THEIR FRIENDS

melody prado

First published in Australia by Maxine Prado 2018

Published in collaboration with Publicious Book Publishing
www.publicious.com.au

ISBN 978 0 6482573 0 1 (pbk)

Artwork by Maria and Paula Basile © 2018
Photography from Pexels.com and family archive
Cover illustration by Maria and Paula Basile
Back cover photo by Maxine Prado
Graphic Design by Maxine Prado

For my human Maxine

CONTENTS

"It is a truth universally acknowledged, that a man or a woman in possession of a good home, must be in want of a cat"

Jane Pawsten

I

From Kit to Cat

Advice for cats with low self-esteem

If you are reading this I guess you are having problems

with your human(s)

Chances are...

YOU FORGOT YOUR CAT POWER

So let me remind you of it

Did
you know
in Ancient Egypt
all cats were revered
and adored? And one of
their most worshipped idols
was a cat Goddess called Bastet?

Sorry, Cat Haters, Science Isn't On Your Side | Popular Science

Why Do So Many People Like Cats?

catpeoplemagazine.com/

1000+

ideas

about Cats

on

Pinterest

Cat - Wikipedia

CAT CAFE MELBOURNE

ADOPTING A CAT OR KITTEN | RSPCA AUSTRALIA

FACECAT | Facebook

Cat Behavior: 17 Things Your Cat Wants to Tell You

Cat Supplies | Amazon.com

Cats are just the funniest pets ever - Funny cat compilation - YouTube

List o actresses who played Cat Woman

Caring for Cats - PETA

CAT PRODUCTS & SUPPLIES ONLINE

Cats of Instagram (@cats_of_instagram)

C A T Protection

Tabby Cat - Chrome Web Store - Google

We are still adored in today's world!

CAT entries on Google at the time

I was typing this page:

2.220.000.000

Clearly, humans are obsessed with us!

TRIVIA TIME

What is the greatest ever musical about?

a - Dogs (as if...)

b - Hamsters (MOL*)

c - Cats

*Meowing Out Loud

Some great
CATS IN LITERATURE

The **Cheshire** cat
Alice in Wonderland by Lewis Carroll

The Old Possum's Book of **Practical Cats**
by T. S. Eliot (on which the musical Cats is based)

Puss in Boots by Charles Perrault

The Cat in the Hat by Dr. Seuss

The Tale of **Tom Kitten** by Beatrix Potter

Just a few

CARTOON CATS HUMANS L♥VE

The Aristocats by Walt Disney

Felix the Cat by Sullivan & Messmer

Garfield by Jim Davies

Sylvester by Friz Freleng

Tom from Tom and Jerry by Hanna Barbera

Top Cat and his gang by Hanna Barbera

etc etc etc...

MOVIE STAR CATS
And the nominees are...

Bob for A Street Cat Named Bob
Based on the book by James Bowen

Cat for Breakfast at Tiffany's
Based on the book by Truman Capote

Mrs Norris for Harry Potter Series
Based on the books by J. K. Rowling

Grumpy Cat for Worst Christmas Ever
Written by Tim Hill and Jeff Morris

Mr. Jinx for Meet the Parents
Written by Jim Herzfeld & John Hamburg

Snowbell for Stuart Little
Based on the book by E. B. White

ICONIC CATS

Kitty Purry, companion of Katy Perry, **Meredith**, companion of Taylor Swift, and so many others... but **Choupette** is the epitome of style, sophistication and cat power! She has two maids and makes millions of euros

If she could win Karl Lagerfeld's love, not to mention thousands of human followers, you can certainly entice the one who lives with you

After reading all the previous pages, I hope you now

realize you are

Powerful

Graceful

Independent

&

Smart

Not to mention **very very** cute!

Hmm...

maybe the problem is not you

It is **THEM!**

II

When your human is just not that into you!

Are you the background picture on your

human's smart device?

Does your human look for you the instant they get home?

Are your accessories fancy?

Have you got any personalised items?

(As you can see, I have a pillow especially made for me)

Do you get several cuddles every day?

If you answered NO to more than

two questions, I hate to tell you but...

Your human is

just not that into you

No need to worry!

I am going to reveal my golden rule

to be adored by humans and get them to do

absolutely everything you want!

It is the one thing you should take from this book:

ALWAYS BE CUDDLEABLE!!!

Do unexpected cat things and deliver cute poses

(But make them seem effortless)

I suggest you make yourself

cat-delicious

and wait at the gate for your human

to get home from work

(Be prepared for lots of cuddles from passers-by)

Do that for two moon cycles, and then every time

your human gets home, make sure you are seen

on the neighbour's fence instead of your own

Charming the neighbours and threatening

to move next door never fails to make you wanted

III

How to get your human out of bed in the morning

That human of yours insists on sleeping when you need

attention, breakfast and access to the outdoor restroom

(Not necessarily in that order)

Most humans tend to ignore our morning meowing and if you just lie down with them you could be waiting for a very long time...

I recommend a **foolproof** three step method

First, walk over the tummy area to remind them that

they too may need the bathroom

Second, apply a few gentle taps on the face

(Retract your claws - scratching your human right now

is not a good idea)

Third, meow in their ear

Repeat these three steps until you succeed

In case of
EMERGENCY ONLY

Upgrade to the door scheme:

From inside the bedroom, push the door until it closes;

then scratch that door desperately, like you urgently

need to go to the bathroom

There is nothing scarier for humans than a wet floor

first thing in the morning

Your human will get up and very likely apologise to you for having closed the door by mistake

WARNING: this strategy is to be used rarely or your human will figure out **YOU** are the one closing the door

IV

How to be fed what you want

whenever you want

Your human should know cats need their routine

The best way to remind a human who forgets about your meal times is to sit beside your empty plate and

scream

For a well-trained human like mine, a stare is enough

Not that you are a glutton, the last time you got a snack

was 3 hours ago!!!

No matter how hungry...

DON'T EVER TOUCH FAKE FOOD!

Better starve for a day than eat something bad

for the rest of your life

You are supposed to eat good quality, real meat!!!

If you don't like it, don't eat it!

(FYI humans return bad meals in restaurants)

Your human will resist at first, but let

the most stubborn (**YOU**) win!

It is always worthwhile to pester dinner guests

Most people will be worried that the poor cat is not getting enough food and some juicy pieces of meat will be sent your way

It is equally effective to show up at the top of the fence when the neighbours are cooking their barbecue and use all your feline allure

V

How to get top service
from your human

Reject everything that smells low quality

Humans are well aware we cats are

high maintenance creatures

Don't like your cat litter?

Do your business elsewhere...

Your cat bed should be clean, comfortable,

inviting and...

...your blanket should be fluffy like a Persian kitten

Otherwise take your other bed,

AKA your human's bed

Sometimes humans give us silly toys

They don't seem to understand it is **sooo** much more fun to play with their stuff

What about those ridiculous devices

for filing your claws? Totally unnecessary

That's what the carpet is for!!!

Now, that is what I call top service,

your **very own** first class window seat!

(Dirty paw prints on the windowsill will get you one)

VI

How to deal with your human's unfriendly friends

So your human has a friend who is not exactly

a cat person

Probably one who believes the myth that cats

do not love their humans like dogs do

You have every right to be annoyed!

Especially if the undesirable shows up when you are

watching your favourite thriller, A Cat in Paris*

*French animated movie written by Alain Gagnol

The intruder takes the lounge, changes the channel

and worse... seems immune to your charm

Always be prepared for visitors

A cat must be aware of all movement

in the house

The Internet is filled with stories of superhero cats risking their lives to save humans from dog attacks, gas leaks, fires and other life-threatening situations

I suggest that whenever the anti-cat is at the door, quickly google heroic cats and leave it where it can be seen

Or place this book on the coffee table,

strategically open at the next page

Here is a list of the type of people who
disliked cats:

Genghis Kahn

Julius Cesar

Napoleon Bonaparte

Benito Mussolini

Adolph Hitler

Not exactly a bunch of nice guys

to be compared to, huh?

If they are not smart enough to get the hint, just hang out with better company until they leave

VII

How to win the boyfriend/girlfriend

And then
THERE WERE THREE...

There is someone lying in bed with your human

and it is **NOT** you!

Guess what?

Your human is mating!

The sooner you mark your territory the better

Make it clear to the stranger:

That bed is **YOUR** bed!

If you share the house with other cats,

unite forces

The more the merrier!

Is the outsider a cat lover?

If not, you need to conquer this person before

they show up with luggage

YES,

this nutcase could be moving into YOUR home soon!

Piece of fish cake!

They desperately need to win you over in order to impress your human and close the deal

Go ahead. Let them try, but play difficult at first

Whenever they call you, don't move, make

an unhappy face and just stare!

If the lover is still around after a complete moon cycle,

the "I prefer you" routine is in order

Next time the couple are on the couch, instead of

choosing your human's lap, go straight to the outsider

and POL*

No one can resist the appeal of being

the favourite

*Purr Out Loud

VIII

How to deal with dogs, kids, baths and other unpleasant things

Not all dogs are bad

If you happen to like the one in your home, you should still keep the upper paw to remind them

who is the boss

The very same principle applies to the kids

T-shirt Copyright © Maxine Prado 2018

What about other people's mean kids?

When provoked,

show some cattitude and HOL*

After all, are you a cat or a rat?

*Hiss Out Loud

Remember trees,

primitive form of furniture?

Better to use them to file your claws in case your human

gets upset when you scratch the sofa and decide to

(horror of horrors) trim them!

Don't

ever

lose

your

best

defence!

If you made the mean kids cry,

there is only one thing to do:

Disappear!

The roof is a cat's best friend...

The cleaners show up?

Pretend you are one of the toys

(They never bother dusting under them)

No stuffed toys in the house?

No access to the roof?

Every cat must have **at least three**

impossible to discover hiding spots

Choose yours!

Coming back to your claws, they can be a handy tool

to keep you safe from baths too

Ah, about that...don't be a dog! Do not parade

in front of your human with dirty fur

Lick yourself, cat!

And please throw up on the grass, never inside

the house or in the presence of your human

They will panic and next thing you will be

on your way to the vet

By the way, the best tactic to avoid the vet is to get your cuddles because...

Three cuddles a day

Keeps the vet away!!!

IX

The art of impressing humans

Little tricks with great impact

Your human needs to play frequently

Even when you are exhausted, entertain them

Pose like a model for their pics, they enjoy showing you off on social media

I know, I know, some of us hate the camera but the truth is the camera loves us!

I call this posture
"the tiger on the tree"

It instantly makes your human fall back in love with you

when you do something they disapprove of

Sleep like a human,

they find it irresistible

What I mean is

sleep like YOUR human

High five your human

I don't know why but they love it

(No claws please)

Always practice the golden rule

Be cuddleable!

Be cuddleable!

Be cuddleable!

And finally,

When things seem difficult,

do not despair

Remember...

MEOW

and

you shall receive!!!

Purring **O**ut **L**oud to
(AKA Acknowledgments)

Andy McDermott from Publicious for valuable guidance

Maria and Paula Basile for wonderful illustrations and feedback

Pexel photographers for great quality, beautiful cat images

Sally Fitzpatrick for revising the material

The Prado family for lovely photos of my relatives

Paul for those cuddles

Maxine, for letting me using her laptop and inspiring me

to do this book, love you

IMAGE CREDITS

All illustrations by artists Maria and Paula Basile

All photos from Pexels.com except the ones listed below,

which are from the family archive